STERLING CHILDREN'S BOOKS
New York

An Imprint of Sterling Publishing
387 Park Avenue South
New York, NY 10016

STERLING CHILDREN'S BOOKS and the distinctive Sterling Children's Books
logo are trademarks of Sterling Publishing Co., Inc.

© 2013 by Sterling Publishing Co., Inc.
Design by Jennifer Browning

All rights reserved. No part of this publication may be reproduced, stored in
a retrieval system, or transmitted, in any form or by any means, electronic,
mechanical, photocopying, recording, or otherwise, without prior written
permission from the publisher.

ISBN 978-1-4027-8430-9

Library of Congress Cataloging-in-Publication Data Available

Distributed in Canada by Sterling Publishing
c/o Canadian Manda Group, 165 Dufferin Street
Toronto, Ontario, Canada M6K 3H6
Distributed in the United Kingdom by GMC Distribution Services
Castle Place, 166 High Street, Lewes, East Sussex, England BN7 1XU
Distributed in Australia by Capricorn Link (Australia) Pty. Ltd.
P.O. Box 704, Windsor, NSW 2756, Australia

For information about custom editions, special sales, and premium and corporate
purchases, please contact Sterling Special Sales at 800-805-5489
or specialsales@sterlingpublishing.com.

Printed in China
Lot #:
2 4 6 8 10 9 7 5 3 1
01/13

www.sterlingpublishing.com/kids

SILVER PENNY STORIES

Goldilocks and the Three Bears

Told by Diane Namm
Illustrated by Stephanie Graegin

Once upon a time there were three bears. There was Papa Bear, a great big bear. There was Mama Bear, a medium-size bear. And there was Baby Bear, a teeny-tiny bear.

Every morning, Papa Bear smoothed
the sheets on his great big bed.
Mama Bear tucked in the blanket
on her medium-size bed. Baby Bear
fluffed the pillows on his
teeny-tiny bed.

Then Papa Bear sat in his great big chair. Mama Bear sat in her medium-size chair. Baby Bear wriggled into his teeny-tiny chair. Mama Bear poured porridge into each of their bowls.

"This porridge is too hot," said Papa Bear in a great big voice.

"Let's leave it to cool by the windowsill," said Mama Bear in a medium-size voice.

"Can we go for a walk while we wait?" asked Baby Bear in a teeny-tiny voice.

So the three bears went for a walk in the woods. No sooner had they gone into the forest than a little girl named Goldilocks walked into their yard.

"What a pretty cottage," she exclaimed. "I wonder who lives here."

Goldilocks stepped inside.

"Is anyone home?" she called.

There was no reply.

Then she saw the porridge bowls cooling by the window.

"I'm hungry," Goldilocks said. "I'm sure no one will mind."

Goldilocks dipped a spoon into Papa Bear's great big bowl. She wrinkled her nose.

"This porridge is much too hot," she said.

Goldilocks tried Mama Bear's medium-size bowl.

"This porridge is much too cold," she said.

Goldilocks tasted the porridge
in Baby Bear's teeny-tiny bowl.

"Ah," she smiled, licking her lips.
"This one is just right!"

Goldilocks gobbled up every
single drop.

Goldilocks sat in Papa Bear's great big chair. She wiggled and squiggled.

"This chair is much too hard," she said.

Goldilocks sat in Mama Bear's medium-size chair. She squiggled and wiggled.

"This chair is much too soft," she said.

Goldilocks bounced onto Baby Bear's teeny-tiny chair.

"Ah," she said. "This one is just right!"

Just then, the chair broke into pieces.

"Oh, where will I rest now?" Goldilocks cried.

Goldilocks found the bedroom. She hopped into Papa Bear's great big bed. She tossed and turned.

"This bed is much too hard," she said.

Goldilocks hopped into Mama Bear's medium-size bed. She turned and tossed.

"This bed is much too soft," she said.

Goldilocks fluffed the pillows on Baby Bear's teeny-tiny bed and hopped in.

"Ah," she said with a big yawn. "This one is just right!"

Goldilocks fell asleep right away.

The three bears came back to the cottage hungry and tired. They picked up their bowls of porridge and were just about to eat when . . .

"Someone's been eating my porridge!" roared Papa Bear.

"Someone's been eating *my* porridge!" growled Mama Bear.

"Someone's been eating *my* porridge and ate it all up!" cried Baby Bear.

The bears were so upset, they had to sit down.

"Someone's been sitting in my chair!" roared Papa Bear.

"Someone's been sitting in *my* chair!" growled Mama Bear.

"Someone's been sitting in *my* chair and broke it all to pieces!" cried Baby Bear.

Now they were even more upset. They had to lie down.

"Someone's been sleeping in my bed!" roared Papa Bear.

"Someone's been sleeping in *my* bed!" growled Mama Bear.

"Someone's been sleeping in *my* bed— and there she is!" cried Baby Bear.

Goldilocks woke up and saw the three unhappy bears.

In a flash, she hopped out of bed and ran out the door before the bears could stop her.

From that day on, the bears always locked their cottage door. And Goldilocks was never seen in the forest again.

E NAMM   MNT
Namm, Diane.
Goldilocks and the three bears /

MONTROSE

06/14

Friends of the
Montrose Public Library